MW01052808

Jackson M. Smith

Jamie Smith

Finley Finds Heaven

Written by
Jackson McLeod Smith
and Janie Smith

Illustrated by
Gail Butler

First Printing

Copyright 2015 by Cavalier Adventures, LLC

All rights reserved. No part of this book may be reproduced or transmitted in any form or by any means, electronically or mechanically, including photocopying, recording, or by any information storage and retrieval system, without written permission.

Authors
Jackson McLeod Smith
Janie Smith
www.finleyfindsheaven.com

Illustrator
Gail Butler
www.gail-butler@fineartamerica.com

Publisher
Wayne Dementi
Dementi Milestone Publishing, Inc.
Manakin-Sabot, VA 23103
www.dementimilestonepublishing.com

The Library of Congress Control Number: 2015955531

ISBN: 978-0-9969157-1-7

Cover design and page layout by:
Charles B. Lindsay

Printed in the United States

A full good faith effort has been made to trace copyright holders and to obtain their permission for use of copyright material. The publisher apologizes for any omissions or errors and would appreciate notification of any corrections that should be incorporated in future reprints or editions of this book.

Our book

is dedicated to:

Our beloved Cavalier, Finley,

who brought us

so many wonderful memories

Janie's husband and Jackson's grandfather,

Daniel McLeod Smith, Sr.

who left this world far too soon

My name is Finley.
I am a Cavalier King Charles Spaniel.

Raleigh and Buster are my brothers.
We all lived with Dan, Anna, and Jackson,
a third grader.

It was so much fun living together as a family. Let me tell you about the fun we had. Jackson always had a great costume at Halloween. He dressed up like a golfer, train engineer, ninja, and a pirate but the wizard was my favorite.

Anna dressed us in costumes, too. One time we were a bumblebee, a pumpkin, and a pig. We had the most fun when she dressed us as three amigos. We were ready to go "bark-or-treating."

Jackson and our parents liked to take fun trips together. Before leaving for vacation, they took Raleigh, Buster, and me to Camp Paws Resort. The camp was an endless day of puppy play.

We could swim in pools, sniff new friends,
and cuddle with friendly counselors.

We even had our own living space with a comfy sofa and a flat screen TV. Barking at animal commercials was something I like to do.

We liked our new friends at camp and
we were always so proud to bring home
our glowing report cards.

One cool November afternoon I was playing in the backyard with my busy brothers. Buster was searching the bushes for butterflies. Raleigh was sniffing under the deck; he was hoping to find some leftovers from last night's cookout.

I was patrolling our fences and
yapping at our neighbors as the family protector.

Then, Anna called us in for dinner.
Buster and Raleigh raced to the backdoor
and went into the kitchen.

Since the air was so sweet and crisp, I just
felt like running. I ran and ran in big circles.
When Anna called me for the third time,
I knew it was time to head inside.

Buster and Raleigh had almost finished their dinner
by the time Anna gave me my dish. My brothers love
to gobble up their meals and treats while I prefer to
enjoy every bite. I like to eat my meals with my paws
wrapped around the bowl.

As I finished my dinner, a strange feeling came over me. I got up on all four paws, tumbled over and everything turned black. The next thing I knew, I was walking through a magical gate. Where was I?

Looking down on Earth, I watched Anna picking me up off the floor and carrying me to her car. Jackson jumped into the back seat and they sped off. They drove quickly to my veterinarian's clinic. You see, my heart had been sick and it needed medicine every day to keep beating and to keep me alive.

Anna was crying, but Jackson did not make a sound. He knew his mother was very upset. The vet rushed me into the back room and tried to make my heart beat again. It would not start. Dr. Clara came out into the waiting room to give Anna and Jackson the news that I had died.

When Dan came home from work,
everyone cried big tears.
After the family went to bed,
it seemed like the whole house was very sad.

While Jackson was snuggled in his bunk bed,
he had the most amazing dream.

When Jackson woke up the next morning,
he was happy and excited about his dream.
He dashed into our parents' bedroom
to tell them all about it.

"Finley is fine," he beamed,
"because he is in Heaven with his cousin Josie!"
Josie was a Bassett Hound who once lived
at Jackson's cousins' house.

He told them that I was living in a
fun condo with Josie. It was heavenly.

Jackson told them that our condo had two bedrooms and a "shath" which is a combination of a shower and a bath for dogs.

He also said that I had a triple bunk bed in my room. It is already there for when Raleigh and Buster pass through the magical gate one day.

Anna and Dan wanted to know more about my
new home. He continued to tell them that Josie
and I could now live more like humans. It was all
so magical. Josie had been blind on Earth but was
now reading many books in Heaven.

Now, I spend my time sculpting and painting. Holding the brush in my teeth and putting the paint on the canvas is so messy but so much fun. I just finished a painting of Raleigh that I call the "Dog-a-Lisa."

Josie and I like to eat some human food in our condo. We have eaten chicken fingers, burgers and fries, cheese sticks, and my favorite, chocolate ice cream. Yum, yum! Raleigh and Buster will surely love this part of Heaven.

Anna and Dan were so happy to hear about
Josie and me. They all had a big family hug
on their bed with Raleigh and Buster, too.

A few nights later, Jackson had another dream about me. He could see me running through the open green fields of heaven chasing butterflies. Cavaliers love to chase butterflies. Going for walks outside was one of my favorite times.

I still remember when Dan would gather our leashes for walks. I would howl and do a happy dance. Now, I can breathe the sweet air and stay outside as long as I wish, run in big circles, and feel no pain in my heart.

Other times I was allowed to sleep on the bed with Dan and Anna. It was very comforting when I could cuddle up during thunderstorms. I loved my special times with Anna when she would scoop me up at the end of the day and hold me close to her heart.

One Saturday about a month later, I visited Jackson at a basketball game.

I was invisible and sat on his lap. Only Jackson
knew I was there. He let my family know
I was still okay.

It makes me so happy that Jackson's dreams made my family feel better. One day Raleigh, Buster, and I will run together again in Heaven's beautiful fields and chase butterflies. It is my hope that all pet owners love and care for their pets as my family does.

Anna, Dan, and Jackson have always been so kind to my Cavalier brothers and me. Our memories together still make my tail wag!

Our Inspirations

Jackson McLeod Smith

My numerous dreams about Finley inspired this book. I was very sad when Finley died and miss him a lot but it makes me feel better knowing how much fun he is having in Heaven. I hope this book helps to comfort all kids (and adults too) after losing a pet they love.

Janie Smith

Knowing my son's family so well, I admired how they loved and cared for their Cavaliers. With the loss of Finley, it was the love, joy and hope that Jackson brought back into the home of a grieving family that inspired our book.

Gail Butler

I feel extremely blessed to have been given the opportunity to illustrate this wonderful story. Anyone who has lost a cherished companion knows how much it hurts. When I learned of Jackson's dreams, it brought tears to my eyes and joy to my heart. I was inspired by the love and innocence of a child and his belief in Heaven.